GRISWAT P9-BTM-919

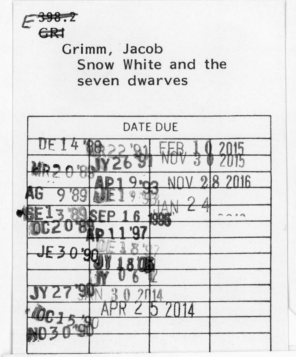

E 398.2
CRI

Grimm, Jacob
Snow White and the
seven dwarves

| DATE DUE | | |
|---|---|---|
| DE 14 '89 | 22 '91 | FEB 10 2015 |
| MR 20 '89 | JY 26 91 | NOV 30 2015 |
| AG 9 '89 | AP 19 '93 | NOV 28 2016 |
| SE 13 '89 | SEP 16 1995 / AN 24 | |
| OC 20 '89 | AP 11 '97 | |
| JE 30 '90 | DE 18 '97 | |
| | JY 18 0 | |
| | JY 06 2 | |
| JY 27 '90 | N 30 2014 | |
| OC 15 '90 | APR 25 2014 | |
| NO 30 '90 | | |

PICTURE BOOK STUDIO USA

The Brothers Grimm

# Snow White

## AND THE SEVEN DWARVES
Illustrated by Chihiro Iwasaki
Translated and adapted by Anthea Bell

Once upon a time in the middle of winter, when the snowflakes were falling like feathers from the sky, a queen sat by her window sewing.

The window had a frame of black ebony, and as the queen sat there with her needlework, looking out at the snow, the needle pricked her finger.

Three drops of blood fell out of the window, and seeing how beautiful
the red looked on the white snow, the queen thought to herself:
Oh, if only I had a child as white as snow, as red as blood, and as black
as the wood of this window frame.

Soon afterwards she had a little daughter who was as white as snow, with lips as red as blood and hair as black as ebony, so she was called Snow White.
Not long after the baby was born, the queen died.

A year later the king married again. The new queen was beautiful, but proud and haughty too, and she could not bear anyone to be lovelier than herself. She had a magic mirror, and when she went to look in this mirror she would say:

"Mirror, mirror on the wall,
Who is fairest of us all?"

And the mirror replied, "O queen, you are the fairest." Then the queen was happy, for she knew that her mirror told the truth.

However, Snow White grew, and became prettier and prettier, and when she was seven years old she was as beautiful as the day, lovelier than the queen herself. So when the queen asked her mirror:

> "Mirror, mirror on the wall,
>  Who is fairest of us all?"

the mirror replied:

> "O Queen, though yours is beauty rare
>  Snow White's a thousand times more fair."

The queen turned quite yellow and green with envy, and from that time on, whenever she set eyes on Snow White, the heart turned over in her body, for she hated the girl so much. And her pride and envy grew and grew like weeds, giving her no rest by day or night.
So she called for a huntsman, and told him, "Take the child out into the forest, kill her, and bring me her liver and lungs to prove that she is dead."

The huntsman obeyed her and took Snow White out to the forest, but when he drew his hunting knife to plunge it into the child's innocent heart, she began to weep, saying, "Oh, dear huntsman, let me live, and I will run away into the forest and never come back." She looked so lovely that the huntsman felt sorry for her, and said,

"Run away then, poor child!" He thought that the wild beasts would soon eat her up, yet he felt as if a weight were lifted from his heart because he need not kill her.

A young wild boar happened to come running by, so the huntsman killed the boar, took out its liver and lungs, and carried them back to the queen, to prove that Snow White was dead. The cook salted them, and prepared them for the table, and the wicked woman ate them, thinking they were Snow White's.

The poor little girl was all alone in the great forest now, and she was so frightened that she looked up at the leaves on the trees, not knowing what to do next. Then she began to run, over sharp stones and through the thorny briars.

The wild animals of the forest ran past her, but they would do nothing to hurt her.

Snow White ran and ran as far as her feet would carry her. At last, when evening came, she saw a little house not far away, and she went inside to rest.

Everything in the house was small, but very neat and clean. There was a table set with seven little plates, seven little spoons, seven little knives and forks and seven little cups, and seven little beds stood by the wall. Snow White was so hungry and thirsty that she ate a few of the vegetables and a little of the bread from each plate, and drank a drop of wine from each cup, so as not to take everything from a single place. Then, feeling very tired, she thought she would rest on one of the little beds, but none of them seemed to fit her: one was too long and another too short, until she came to the last bed, which was just right, and she lay down, said her prayers, and fell asleep.

When it was quite dark, the masters of the house came home.
They were seven dwarves who dug and mined ore in the mountains.
They lit their seven little lanterns, and when it was light in their
house they saw that someone had been there, for the place was not
quite the same as they had left it.

"Who's been sitting in my chair?" said the first.

"Who's been eating from my plate?" said the second.

"Who's taken some of my bread?" said the third.

"Who's eaten some of my vegetables?" said the fourth.

"Who's used my fork?" said the fifth.

"Who's been cutting with my knife?" said the sixth.

"Who's been drinking from my cup?" said the seventh.

Then the first dwarf looked around, and saw a little hollow in his bed. "Who's been lying in my bed?" he asked. And the other dwarves came running and cried, "Somebody's been lying in our beds too!" But when the seventh looked at his bed, he saw Snow White lying there asleep. He called the others, and they came with their lanterns and looked at Snow White. "Oh, what a pretty little girl!" they cried, and they let her sleep on in the little bed, while the seventh dwarf shared a bed with his companions that night, an hour with each of them.

In the morning Snow White woke. She was frightened when she saw the seven dwarves, but they spoke to her kindly, and asked her name. "Snow White," she said, and she told them how her stepmother had wanted to kill her, but the huntsman had spared her life, and how she ran all day until she came to their little house. "If you will look after it for us," said the dwarves, "cook, make the beds, wash and knit and sew and keep the place neat and clean, then you can stay with us, and you will lack for nothing." "Oh yes," said Snow White, "with all my heart." So she stayed with the dwarves, and kept house for them. They went off to the mountains every morning, looking for gold and ore, and when they came home in the evening she had their supper ready. But she was left alone all day, and the good dwarves warned her, "Beware of your stepmother! She will soon find out that you're here, so don't let anybody in."

As for the queen, she felt sure that now she had eaten Snow White's liver and lungs she was the fairest again, so she went to her mirror and asked:        "Mirror, mirror on the wall,
            Who is fairest of us all?"
But the mirror replied:
                "O Queen, you are of beauty rare,
                Yet know you well
                Where the seven dwarves dwell,
                Snow White's a thousand times more fair."

The queen knew that her mirror always told the truth, and she was
afraid, for she realized that the huntsman had tricked her and Snow
White was still alive. So she stained her face, dressed in the clothes
of an old pedlar woman, went over the mountains to the seven
dwarves' house, and knocked on the door, crying, "Good wares to sell,
fine wares to sell!"

When Snow White looked out of the window, she showed her a pretty
comb. Surely I can let this good old woman in, thought Snow White,
so she unbolted the door and bought the comb.

"Now let me comb your hair for you!" said the old woman. However,
she had poisoned the comb by witchcraft, and as soon as it touched
Snow White's head the poison worked and the girl fell lifeless to the floor.

"So much for you!" said the wicked queen, and she went away, sure that
she was the fairest once again.

That evening, when the seven dwarves came home, they were horrified
to see their dear Snow White lying where the queen had left her for dead.
They raised her up, and seeing the comb in her hair, they took it out again.
She came back to her senses, and told them what had happened.
"That old pedlar woman was none other than your wicked stepmother,"
they said. "So be careful, and don't open the door to anyone at all when
we are not with you."

As for the queen, when she came home she looked in her mirror and
asked:          "Mirror, mirror on the wall,
                Who is fairest of us all?"
And the mirror answered, just as before:
                "O Queen, you are of beauty rare,
                Yet know you well,
                Where the seven dwarves dwell,
                Snow White's a thousand times more fair."

Then the queen was very angry. She went to a secret room and made
a poisoned apple, very pretty to look at, with red cheeks, but anyone
who ate the smallest piece of it would die. Next she stained her face,
dressed as a peasant woman with apples to sell, and went over the
mountains to the seven dwarves' house.

When she knocked at the door, Snow White looked out of the window
and said, "I'm not allowed to let anyone in!"
"Well, never mind," said the old woman. "I'll find buyers for my apples
soon enough. Here, I'll give you one!"
"Oh no," said Snow White, "I mustn't take it."
"Why, are you afraid of poison?" asked the old woman. "Look, I'll cut the
apple in two, and you can eat one half and I'll eat the other."
However, the apple was so cunningly made that only half of it was
poisoned. Snow White longed for the pretty apple, and seeing the
peasant woman eat it, she couldn't help putting out her hand to take the

poisoned half. But no sooner had she taken a piece of it in her mouth than she fell down dead.

Then the cruel queen looked at her and laughed, saying, "White as snow, red as blood, black as ebony! The dwarves won't wake you this time!" And when she came home and asked her mirror:

> "Mirror, mirror on the wall,
>   Who is fairest of us all?"

the mirror at last replied, "O queen, you are the fairest."
Then her envious heart was at peace.

When the dwarves came home they found Snow White lying there dead. They raised her up to see if there was any poisonous thing about her, and combed her hair, and washed her in water and wine, but it was no good; the poor child was dead, and would not come to life again.

So they laid her on a bier, and all seven dwarves sat beside it for three days, weeping and mourning. Then they were going to bury her body, but she still looked so fresh and pretty, just as if she were alive, that they said to each other, "How can we put her into the black earth?" And they made a transparent glass coffin, placed her inside it, and wrote her name on the coffin in golden letters, saying that she was a king's daughter.

Then they put the coffin on the mountainside, and the birds and beasts came to mourn Snow White as well. She lay there in her coffin for a long, long time looking as if she were only sleeping, for she was still as white as snow, with lips as red as blood and hair as black as ebony.

One day a king's son came to the forest, and asked for shelter for the
night in the dwarves' house. He saw the coffin on the mountainside,
with Snow White inside it, and read what the golden letters said.
"Let me have this coffin," he begged the dwarves. "I will give you
    anything you ask for it."
"No," said the dwarves. "We wouldn't sell it for all the gold in the world."
"Then give it to me," said the king's son, "for I can't live without
    looking at Snow White, and I will care for her as my dearest treasure."

Hearing this, the dwarves were sorry for him, and gave him the coffin. The king's son told his servants to carry it away on their shoulders, and it so happened that one of them stumbled, and the piece of apple that Snow White had bitten off was jolted out of her throat. In a moment she came back to life, opened her eyes, lifted the lid of the coffin, and sat up.

"Where am I?" she asked.

"With me," said the king's son joyfully, and he told her what had happened. "I love you more than all the world," he said. "Come home to my father's castle, and you will be my wife."

So Snow White agreed to marry him, and their wedding was celebrated with great magnificence.

Now Snow White's wicked stepmother was invited to the wedding, and when she had put her fine clothes on she went to her mirror and said:

> "Mirror, mirror on the wall,
>  Who is fairest of us all?"

And the mirror replied:

> "O Queen, though yours is beauty rare,
>  The bride's a thousand times more fair."

The queen was beside herself with terror, and at first she thought she wouldn't go to the wedding, but then she knew she must see the bride for herself, and when she set eyes on her and recognized Snow White, she was so angry that she fell down dead.

As for Snow White and the king's son, they lived happily ever after.

The cover and jacket design is a combination of 2 individual illustrations.
Illustrations copyright © 1984, Takeshi Matsumoto
Original Japanese edition published in 1984 by Kodansha Ltd., Tokyo.
English text copyright © 1985, Neugebauer Press USA Inc.
Published in USA by Picture Book Studio USA,
an imprint of Neugebauer Press USA, Inc.
Distributed by Alphabet Press, Natick, MA.
Distributed in Canada by Vanwell Publishing, St. Catharines.
Published in U.K. by Neugebauer Press Publishing Ltd., London.
All rights reserved.
Printed in Austria.

LIBRARY OF CONGRESS CATALOGING IN PUBLICATION DATA

Grimm, Jacob, 1785-1863.
Snow White and the seven dwarves.

Translation of: Schneewittchen.
Summary: Retells the tale of the beautiful princess whose lips were red
as blood, skin was white as snow, and hair was as black as ebony.
[1. Fairy tales.  2. Folklore–Germany]
I. Grimm, Wilhelm, 1786-1859.   II. Iwasaki, Chihiro, 1918-1974,
ill. III. Title.
PZ8.G882Sm     1985        398.2'2'0943        85-12158
ISBN 0-88708-012-X

Ask your bookseller for these other PICTURE BOOK STUDIO books
illustrated by Chihiro Iwasaki:
THE RED SHOES by Hans Christian Andersen
THE LITTLE MERMAID by Hans Christian Andersen

And these by the Brothers Grimm:
HANSEL AND GRETEL illustrated by Lisbeth Zwerger